AFRICAN TALES

A BAREFOOT COLLECTION

written by Gcina Mhlophe

illustrated by Rachel Griffin

Barefoot Books
Celebrating Art and Story

Africa has a strong storytelling tradition. The peoples of Africa speak more languages — over a thousand — than those of any other continent. Theirs is a largely spoken culture, with popular wisdom that has been passed on by word of mouth since ancient times, and has given rise to many stories that are still recounted today. These stories explain everything — from the creation of all things, to the reason why owls only come out at night. African storytellers work with praise singers and other musicians, using a call and response technique, in which the audience joins in.

In Africa, and all over the world, stories live through retelling. So why not join in the African tradition of storytelling yourself, and pass these stories along? Now turn the page to begin this remarkable voyage in which you will be amazed by all that is Africa!

You'll notice that each story in this book ends with "*Cosi cosi iyaphela*," which means "Here I rest my story." This is the traditional way that Zulu storytellers end their tales.

Gcina Mhlophe, Durban, 2009

My inspiration for the artwork in this book has come from a variety of sources and influences: from my many wonderful trips to western Africa, from my parents' travels to other African countries, including Malawi and Lesotho, from trawling innumerable African shops and stores throughout the UK, and from countless hours spent in museums and libraries. Each of these has resulted in a treasure trove of mementoes: brightly colored beads or interesting fabrics; fascinating hand-made papers and gorgeous clay pots; photographs of African animals, people, their daily lives and their countries and communities.

I have greatly enjoyed illustrating this book and hope that the result is a wondrous feast for your eyes to gaze upon and wonder at. I also hope that, through the use of different fabrics, beads, papers and colors, I have given you a sense of the magic and diversity that is Africa. Be on the watch for amazing treasures at every turn of the page and — above all — enjoy your travels.

Rachel Griffin, England, 2009

Contents

Welcome to Africa!

THE SECOND LARGEST continent on Earth, Africa is filled with amazing diversity — rich cultures, fascinating peoples, incredible wildlife and vastly differing environments, from the enormous dry Sahara Desert in the north, to the dense rain forests of West and Central Africa, to the rocky Kaapvaal region of the south, rich with diamonds and gold. There are more than fifty independent countries in Africa and on the islands off its coasts. It is surrounded by the Mediterranean Sea, the Atlantic Ocean, the Red Sea and the Indian Ocean, while the Equator runs almost exactly through the middle of the continent.

The history of Africa is as rich and varied as its many cultures. Indeed, it has the longest human history of any continent. Fossils of the earliest humans were found here, along with evidence of bone tools and rock paintings. The first great African civilization began in Egypt in 3400 BC, where it flourished for nearly three thousand years, while important cities also rose up along the banks of the Niger River in West Africa. The merchants of these early African kingdoms relied on trade, traveling great distances over difficult caravan routes through the deserts and plains. The arrival of Europeans in the sixteenth century began with Portuguese exploration of the

coasts of Africa as they looked for a safe route to India, and continued through the nineteenth and much of the twentieth century, with the Dutch, the French and the English. As these Europeans settled in Africa, they formed boundaries that paid no heed to existing local ones and defined colonies under European rule.

In the 1960s — a period known as the "Decade of Independence" — most African nations threw off foreign rule and started governing themselves once again. This brought about a new blossoming of arts and culture as the different countries of Africa began to explore their identities with their newfound freedom.

Today, Africa is a continent where modern universities rise next to ancient pyramids, where wildlife safaris take visitors to explore the rolling plains, where small villages thrive side by side with big cities. Like peoples the world over, those who live in Africa have faced many hardships, including civil war, drought and disease, but despite this they remain strong, supported by their families and wider communities, and delighting in the rich cultures they've nourished since ancient times. Vastly different from north to south, east to west, Africa is a remarkable place, unlike any other on earth.

5

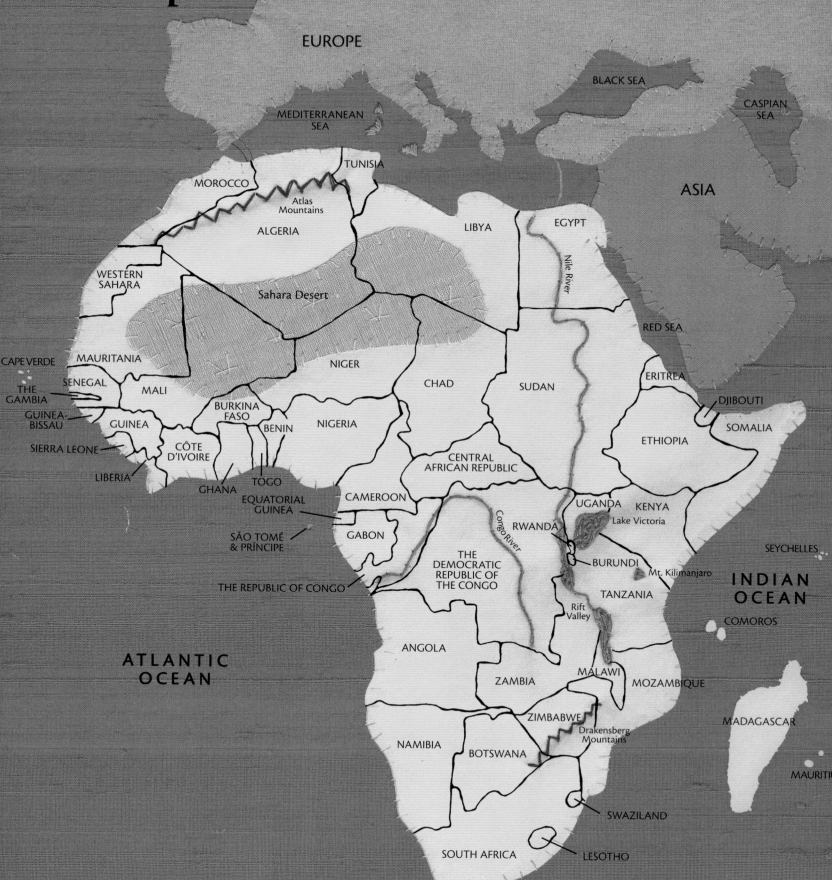

Map of Africa

EUROPE

ASIA

BLACK SEA

CASPIAN SEA

MEDITERRANEAN SEA

TUNISIA

MOROCCO

Atlas Mountains

ALGERIA

LIBYA

EGYPT

Nile River

WESTERN SAHARA

Sahara Desert

RED SEA

CAPE VERDE

MAURITANIA

NIGER

CHAD

SUDAN

ERITREA

DJIBOUTI

SENEGAL

THE GAMBIA

MALI

BURKINA FASO

SOMALIA

GUINEA-BISSAU

GUINEA

BENIN

NIGERIA

CENTRAL AFRICAN REPUBLIC

ETHIOPIA

SIERRA LEONE

CÔTE D'IVOIRE

LIBERIA

GHANA

TOGO

CAMEROON

UGANDA

KENYA

Lake Victoria

EQUATORIAL GUINEA

RWANDA

SÃO TOMÉ & PRÍNCIPE

GABON

Congo River

BURUNDI

SEYCHELLES

Mt. Kilimanjaro

THE REPUBLIC OF CONGO

THE DEMOCRATIC REPUBLIC OF THE CONGO

TANZANIA

INDIAN OCEAN

COMOROS

Rift Valley

ATLANTIC OCEAN

ANGOLA

MALAWI

MOZAMBIQUE

MADAGASCAR

ZAMBIA

NAMIBIA

ZIMBABWE

Drakensberg Mountains

MAURITI

BOTSWANA

SWAZILAND

SOUTH AFRICA

LESOTHO

* Geologically, Africa is one of the oldest continents. The first human beings evolved here millions of years ago.

* The Sahara is the world's largest hot desert. It is over 3,500,000 square miles in size, and covers most of northwest Africa.

* The Nile is the longest river in the world. It is over four thousand miles in length, and it flows from Central Africa to the Mediterranean Sea.

* The highest mountain in Africa, snowcapped Mount Kilimanjaro, is in the Eastern Highlands.

* Africa has the most varied wildlife in the world. It is also home to some of the largest populations of wild animals, including lemurs, wildebeest, antelopes and hyenas.

* The Great Pyramid of Giza in Egypt is one of the Seven Wonders of the World and is the largest pyramid ever built.

* The predominant arts and crafts forms in Africa are masks and figurines, often used in religious ceremonies. Wood is one of the most frequently used materials.

* Typical African musical instruments include drums, xylophones, rattles, clappers, bamboo flutes and ivory trumpets. While European musicians were developing ideas about harmony, Africans were developing rhythm, creating the most sophisticated percussive arrangements in the world.

Namibia

NAMIBIA IS BORDERED by Angola and Zambia in the north, Botswana in the east, South Africa in the south, and the chilly Atlantic Ocean in the west. The country is very different from north to south and east to west. It is divided into five geographical regions, each with distinctive conditions. There are dusty deserts — including the Kalahari Desert and the Namib Desert, from which the country takes its name — sand dunes and rock formations, dry savannah and scrubby woodland, and lush forests.

There are not many people in Namibia because of the harsh conditions and lack of water in many places. Despite this, it is home to ten tribes: Owambo, Kavango, Caprivians, Herero, Himba, Damara, Nama, Topnaars, Tswana and San. The San are nomadic hunters and gatherers, and practice traditional healing. The San women harvest and prepare medicinal plants for treating many different sicknesses, like Nolwandle — our heroine in the next story — learns to do from her adoptive parents.

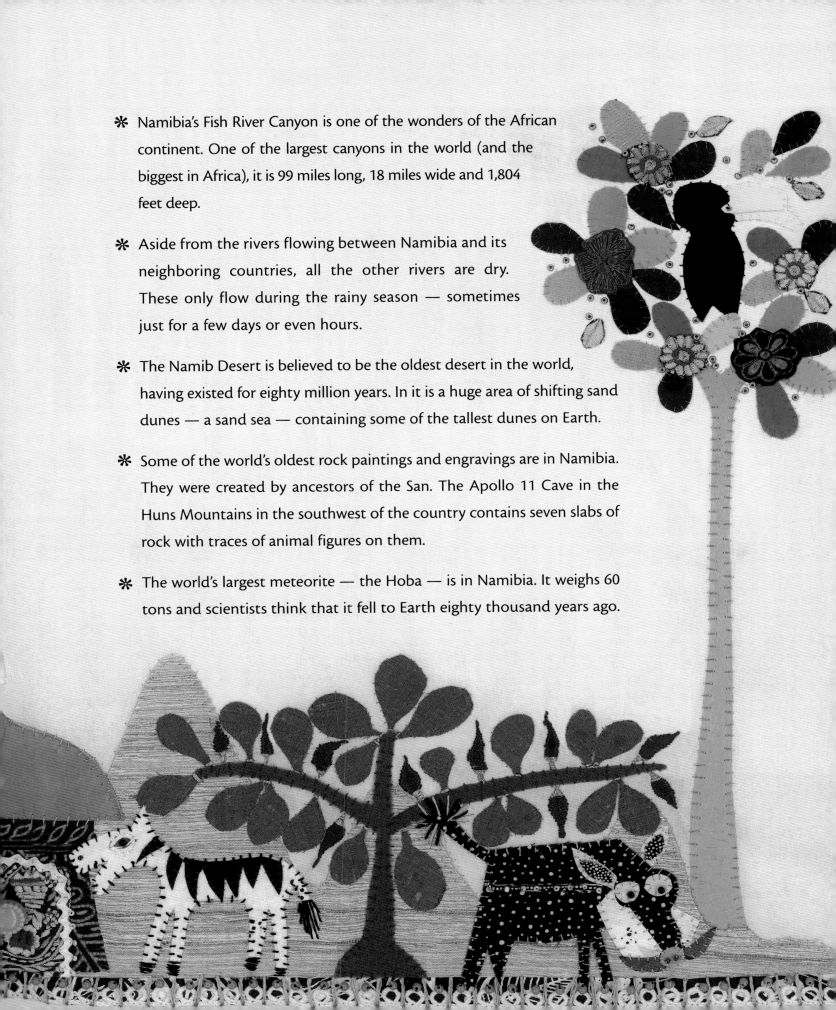

* Namibia's Fish River Canyon is one of the wonders of the African continent. One of the largest canyons in the world (and the biggest in Africa), it is 99 miles long, 18 miles wide and 1,804 feet deep.

* Aside from the rivers flowing between Namibia and its neighboring countries, all the other rivers are dry. These only flow during the rainy season — sometimes just for a few days or even hours.

* The Namib Desert is believed to be the oldest desert in the world, having existed for eighty million years. In it is a huge area of shifting sand dunes — a sand sea — containing some of the tallest dunes on Earth.

* Some of the world's oldest rock paintings and engravings are in Namibia. They were created by ancestors of the San. The Apollo 11 Cave in the Huns Mountains in the southwest of the country contains seven slabs of rock with traces of animal figures on them.

* The world's largest meteorite — the Hoba — is in Namibia. It weighs 60 tons and scientists think that it fell to Earth eighty thousand years ago.

Nolwandle, Girl of the Waves

LONG, LONG AGO, a young girl named Sky lived with her parents in a remote mountain village. During the rainy season she liked nothing better than to sit beside the river at the foot of the mountain, watching and listening to the waters as they flowed joyously to the sea. She had never been to the ocean, but she always dreamed of seeing it one day. Everyone in her village knew that she wanted to live beside the sea more than anything else in the world.

Years passed and Sky grew into a pretty young maiden. Many men tried to win her hand in marriage, but she would not accept any of them. Only a man born near the sea would do for her. At last, Sky's patience was rewarded: she met a man lost in the mountains. It turned out he came from a fishing village on the coast.

As soon as the two of them set eyes on each other, they fell in love. The wedding ceremony took place in Sky's village, and then the young couple went back to the man's home together. They loved each other

very much, and Sky loved the sea too, just as much as she had always imagined she would. She could not thank her ancestors enough for such a gift.

But Sky's mother-in-law would not have anything to do with her. She thought that Sky should have stayed in the mountains and married someone from her own village. She refused to help her get used to her new life and when the girl gave birth to an adorable baby daughter, she did not take any notice of the child either. So every day, the young mother took her little daughter with her when she went to tend the goats or work on the family's small plot of land. When the heat of the sun became unbearable she would go to the water's edge and sing to the waves, asking them to look after her baby daughter while she worked. She sang her song and the waves promptly reached out and received the baby. Sky called her baby Nolwandle, Girl of the Waves, and this is the song she sang each day:

> *"Magagasi olwandle … Waves of the Sea,*
> *Nansi ingane yami … Here is my child.*
> *Ngigcineleni yona … Please look after her for me*
> *Mina ngiyosebensa … While I go to work."*

11

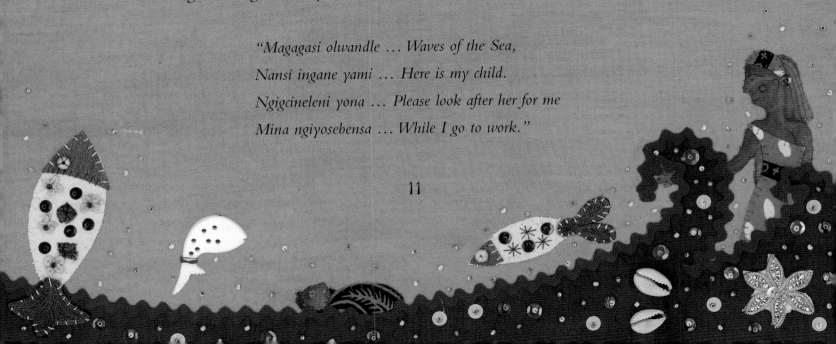

Every day, Sky left Nolwandle with the waves. When her work was done she came back to the beach and sang a different song for the return of her baby. Then the waves brought Nolwandle back and mother and daughter went home. This arrangement went on until Nolwandle was three years old. Then, one cool autumn morning, Nolwandle was playing in the waves as usual when the sea took her further and further away from her home shore. When her mother finished her work and came looking for her, Nolwandle was nowhere to be seen.

Sky sang and sang to the sea, frantically running up and down the beach. When she realized that her daughter was lost, she cried herself to exhaustion and fainted on the sand. That is where she was found by her husband later that evening. Both of them were heartbroken. They could only imagine that their daughter had drowned.

However, although Nolwandle had disappeared, she was actually quite safe. The sea carried her to an island a few hours away from her home.

A childless old couple found her on the beach while they were gathering seaweed. And this was no ordinary old pair — both husband and wife were well-known and respected healers. They brought the lost child up as their own, with much love, and they, too, called her Nolwandle.

Nolwandle, Girl of the Waves

The little girl was welcomed by the small community of the island and she came to know a lot about the healing herbs that her adoptive parents used. As they grew older, they relied on her more and more. Nolwandle spent many of her days looking for the right herbs and helping her new mother and father prepare medicines for their patients. She learned fast, and by the time she was fifteen years old, she had been taught everything the old couple knew.

Late one windy night, when the frail old couple felt that death was near, they spoke to Nolwandle gently. "Dear child, you must try to find your real parents again. We will soon be on our way to join our ancestors."

"But I have been so happy here with you!" cried Nolwandle. "I do not even know where I came from, so how could I find my parents?"

"Trust the great ocean that brought you to us when you were so small and defenseless. Nothing harmed you then, and nothing will harm you now," said the old man knowingly. "Let the sea take you where you need to go."

That night, none of them could sleep. They sang the old songs that many healers sing to connect with the ancestral world. In the hour before dawn, they stood together on the beach holding hands, waiting for the sun to rise. At last, the eastern sky turned orange and the birds began to sing, greeting the new day. Carrying a large bag

of herbs and all the knowledge the old couple had shared with her over the years, Nolwandle stepped bravely into the sea. The magical waves came bounding happily to her and quickly bore her away. Nolwandle could not imagine what her life would be like without the adoptive mother and father she so loved, but she knew she had to look forward. She had to place her trust in the great ocean and hope that it would carry her back to her home village.

The sea was cold and wild. Nolwandle struggled to hold on to her precious bag. Unable to tell which way she was going, she desperately scanned the horizon for signs of dry land, but the waves tossed her all over the place and she could see nothing but ocean. In the end she let herself be carried by the currents. All at once her fear disappeared and she felt a gentle sense of peace come over her. She closed her eyes, lay on the bag of herbs and drifted in and out of sleep.

It was almost nightfall when Nolwandle was washed up on to a beach. Not far away, children were playing and swimming happily. She greeted them and asked if they had ever heard of a girl called Nolwandle.

"You mean the one the old people talk about all the time?" one boy asked.

"What do they say?"

"Don't you know? They say that she was given to the sea by her mother because she had no one to help her with the baby. Then one day the ocean took her away and she never came back."

The girl who spoke eyed the soaking-wet stranger suspiciously.

Nolwandle thanked the children and asked them to show her which hut that woman lived in. Dripping wet and very tired, she picked up her heavy load and walked toward it. The group of children watched her, puzzled by what they had seen and heard.

Nolwandle was lucky. She found her home, but she also found that her mother was lying in bed, very sick. There was no time for her to rest — she had to work fast. She searched in her bag of herbs to find the right medicine and sat at her mother's bedside for three days and three nights.

Slowly, the medicine worked its magic and her mother's health returned. Of course, Sky's heart sang with joy at having her beloved Nolwandle back home again. It took Nolwandle many days to tell her parents about the time she had spent on the island where the ocean had taken her. She told them, too, about the wonderful old couple who had loved her and looked after her, and groomed her into a powerful young healer.

Listening to Nolwandle, Sky's mother-in-law was ashamed in her old age to learn that total strangers had shown so much love to

16

Nolwandle, Girl of the Waves

her grandchild, whom she had so neglected. She silently vowed that she would change her ways and give her family all the love she could. So, at last, everyone could enjoy being together as a family.

Nolwandle lived for many years, using her knowledge of herbs to help the people who came to her from far and wide. Her learning was passed on to future generations, and her fame as a healer still lives on.

Cosi cosi iyaphela
Here I rest my story.

Malawi

MALAWI IS A long and narrow country in the southeast. It is known as the "Warm Heart of Africa" because of its friendly people. Landlocked between Zambia, Mozambique and Tanzania, Malawi lies within the Great Rift Valley.

The climate in Malawi is subtropical, with a rainy season running from November to April, and virtually no rain for the rest of the year — much like the drought experienced by Makhosi's people in this next story.

Music and dance are an integral part of Malawian culture, the most popular forms of music being gospel, reggae, hip-hop and kwela (see next page). For the Chewa people of Malawi, dance and music are particularly important. Gule Wamkulu, the ritual dance performed on special occasions, is one of the oldest forms of dance in Malawi. Male dancers with masks representing wild animals and the spirits of the dead each play a different evil character in order to teach moral and social values to the audience. Like Makhosi's magic-horn song, music in Malawi is clearly more than just entertainment.

✳ Spiritual songs are very popular in Malawi, not just at religious ceremonies, but also as entertainment or to accompany everyday tasks. These are mostly sung "a cappella" (without musical instruments), or with just a drumbeat.

✳ The Kasambwe Brothers are a popular Malawian music group. Formed in 1987, they use guitars, homemade drums and other unusual percussion instruments including one fashioned from the branch of a tree, a string of bottle tops and old bicycle parts. Their music usually centers around the themes of love, life and duty.

✳ Kwela, a type of street music similar to jazz, became popular in Malawi in the 1960s and was important to the development of Malawian music in general. The word "kwela" is Zulu for "get up" and its rhythms make you want to do exactly that!

✳ Malawi has thirty thousand traditional healers in its villages and towns. Many of the people in rural areas use traditional medicine for their ailments.

✳ Rainmakers, like Makhosi's uncle in the story "Makhosi and the Magic Horns," use rituals (a symbolic set of actions) to control the environment, such as burning particular kinds of wood to influence the movement of the clouds.

Makhosi and the Magic Horns

A LONG TIME AGO, when the world was still young and magic happened more often than it happens today, there lived a boy called Makhosi. He was handsome and hard-working, and his parents were proud of the way he took such good care of their large herd of animals. Most of his friends were herd boys too, and they spent their days out in the open, taking their animals to the best grazing places.

Of course, when the rains came and the grass was lush and plentiful, the boys also had lots of time to talk, play games, discuss their dreams and enjoy the beauty of the countryside. But in the dry season, they had to walk a long way to find new pastures. Most of them hated this, but Makhosi regarded it as an adventure to go traveling on his own and explore new places, meet other people, hear their stories and learn about their customs.

Well, Makhosi's chance to do this came sooner than he had expected. The land suffered a long drought, and with the drought came a strange new sickness.

There was panic in the villages as more and more animals and people fell ill. First, they grew dizzy, then their muscles weakened and their eyelids became so heavy that they could hardly keep them open. Animals dropped where they stood and refused to get up again. Some of the cows whose calves had died lowed for hours, and their sorrowful cries were almost unbearable. The people called on their most respected herbalists and healers to help them but no one could find a cure.

One day, both Makhosi's parents fell ill. He was sad and scared and very confused — whom should he take care of, his parents or the cattle?

"Oh, how I wish my dear uncle were here! He would know what to do," said Makhosi that evening with a deep sigh.

His parents heard him. "Son, it is time for us to make a very serious decision. Come and sit here with us," his mother said.

"Mama, did you hear me? I am sorry — I did not mean to disturb you."

"No, you did not disturb us. We were not sleeping; it is just our eyes…" said his father from the mat where he was resting.

"Listen, Makhosi," continued his mother. "Earlier today your father and I were talking. We agree that you should wake up very early tomorrow morning and travel to my brother's home. It's safer there. I do not want you to get sick too."

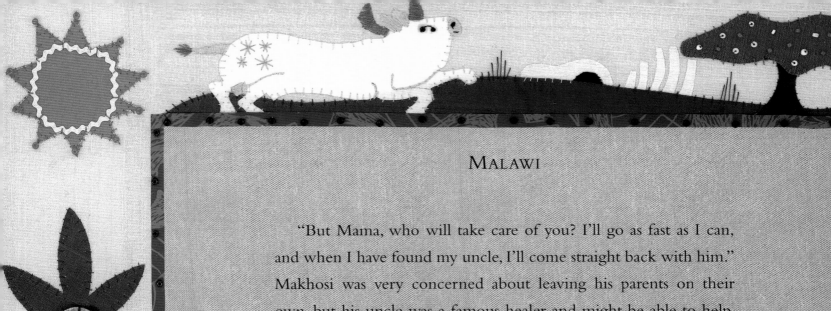

MALAWI

"But Mama, who will take care of you? I'll go as fast as I can, and when I have found my uncle, I'll come straight back with him." Makhosi was very concerned about leaving his parents on their own, but his uncle was a famous healer and might be able to help, even though other healers had failed.

"You must take the white bull to ride," said his father, holding Makhosi's hand very tight. "It is a long way to walk, but with the bull it will only take one day and one night. The white bull is special. It will help you with any problems you may have on the way. When you get there, tell your uncle everything and he will think of a plan."

"I understand, Baba, but what about you, and what about the cattle?"

"My eyes may be closed, but something tells me the rains will be here in a few weeks. Some of our cattle will survive. And I do not plan to die yet. What about you — Mother of Makhosi?" he asked, turning to his wife with a gentle laugh in his voice.

"He, he! If I die, what will become of you, I ask!" She smiled and spoke lightly, as if she found the whole situation quite hilarious. But Makhosi knew they were both trying to be strong for him.

"Fine. I will go," he said quietly.

By sunrise the next morning, Makhosi and the white bull were already far from home. The bull stepped out as if it knew exactly

22

where to go, and it moved at quite a fast pace, too. It was amazingly strong. They kept on for hours, protected from the hot sun by a steady wind. There was so much sadness around. Makhosi could feel it everywhere. Near the parched watering holes they passed lay the dry bones of dead animals, and above them vultures were circling lazily. For a while, the birds followed the bull and the young boy. Then they gave up and flew away.

Only when the two friends had left the vultures behind and were heading for the distant mountains did the bull show any signs of tiredness. So Makhosi found a lonely, leafless tree and sat under its flimsy shade. He took out dried meat sticks, mealy bread and some water, and had some lunch. The water he shared with the bull, pouring it into an open calabash.

After Makhosi had eaten, the two companions lay down for a well-deserved rest. They must have slept for an hour or two when they heard the sound of big, heavy feet shaking the very ground they were lying on. Makhosi and the bull sprang up and looked around. A herd of buffaloes was running past them. They seemed very purposeful, so Makhosi wondered if they could smell water somewhere nearby. The young boy was about to get onto the bull's back and follow them when the buffaloes stopped, turned and headed straight toward them.

23

Then the strangest thing happened. The white bull spoke to Makhosi.

"Please do not panic. I will have to fight that buffalo bull. He is strong, and he will kill me. When I am dead, cut off my horns and continue to your uncle's village. Whenever you need something on the way, sing a song and ask the horns to help — they are magic."

"Why don't you use their magic to defeat the buffalo bull?" cried Makhosi in despair. But there was no time for an answer — the herd was upon them. Makhosi had to scramble up the tree for safety.

The two bulls battled it out for some time. Then the white bull fell to the ground and did not move. Only a long, sorrowful bellow came from him as the buffalo herd set off again. A sad Makhosi climbed down from the tree and gently stroked the bull. It took him a while finally to force himself to cut off the horns. He had barely put them in his bag when a great whirlwind circled the body of the bull and took it away.

Just like that, it was gone. Makhosi stood stock still, stunned. Then he turned toward the dusty path that would eventually bring him to his uncle's village.

By the end of the day, Makhosi was exhausted. He headed for a village in the distance and looked for a hut where he could ask for somewhere to sleep. The place was almost deserted, but he found a small hut where a fire was burning. An old woman stood at the door.

"Greetings, Grandmother."

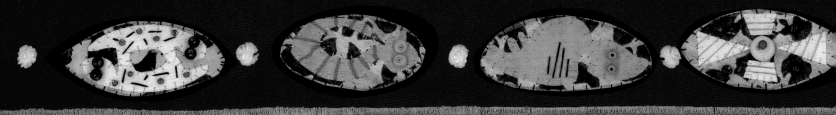

"Greetings to you, too. Where are you traveling to?"

"I am on my way to visit my uncle. The people and animals in my home village are dying and there is great hunger. May I please spend the night here?"

"A place to sleep is no problem, but as for food — I have none. Things have been bad here too." She was as poor as he was, but her smile was so warm it went straight to his heart and Makhosi felt truly welcome. After talking a little about his family and the long drought, he knelt down and took out the white bull's horns, clapping his hands as he sang:

> *"Awe phondo lwami, olwasale mpini phondo lwami.*
> *Awe phondo lwami, awuphake sidle phondo lwami!*
> *Oh, horns of mine, left to me in battle, horns of mine.*
> *Oh, horns of mine, please make food for us to eat, horns of mine!"*

The magic worked. The old woman's big wooden trays were suddenly laden with steaming hot food: tender lamb ribs, steamed bread, sweet potatoes, tasty spinach and creamy milk. They ate gratefully and then fell asleep with full stomachs for the first time in many months.

Early the next morning, Makhosi sang to the horns again and they prepared an enormous breakfast, and enough food for the old woman to eat for many days. When he said goodbye she gave him a warm blanket for the journey. He thanked her for her hospitality and set off again.

MAKHOSI AND THE MAGIC HORNS

The path was straight but Makhosi still had a long way to go. There was no sign of life for some time. Then he came to a region where tall grasses swayed in the wind like a golden ocean. Makhosi's spirits rose, but then suddenly he heard a cry of despair. He followed the sound to a big cave hidden near a dry riverbed. There, he saw a young woman wailing. "My son, my poor son!" she wept.

Makhosi rushed to her side and asked if he could help.

"My son was pulled into this cave by a strange-looking dwarf!" cried the woman. "We had been collecting some clay to make pots. I don't know where the dwarf appeared from or why he has taken my child."

Makhosi quickly took out his magic horns and clapped his hands as he sang:

> *"Awe phondo lwami, olwasale mpini phondo lwami.*
> *Awe phondo lwami, sicela abuye umfana phondo lwami!*
> *Oh, horns of mine, left to me in battle, horns of mine.*
> *Oh, horns of mine, we ask you to return the boy, horns of mine!"*

Again, the magic worked and soon, footsteps could be heard coming from the recesses of the cave. It was the dwarf, carrying the boy in his arms, and placed him at his mother's feet. Suddenly a great whirlwind circled around the dwarf and he was whisked away; just like that — he was gone. The boy threw himself into his mother's arms, who by now was crying tears of joy.

"Oh, how could I ever thank you?" she cried, looking at Makhosi in disbelief. "I thought I had lost my son for ever!"

"These magic horns are a mystery to me, too, but I am happy that I could help. You must be tired, though. How far away is your home?"

Makhosi walked back to their hut with them. When they arrived, he sang to the horns and asked them to make big clay pots for the woman. Again, the magic worked: the pots were beautifully made and brightly decorated. The woman was overjoyed.

But something seemed to have happened. It was taking Makhosi longer than he had expected to reach his uncle's village. He tried to walk faster in the hope of reaching the village by the end of the day, but it was no use. The sun was going to set again. He missed his home and wondered about his parents. Would they be all right while he was away? Yes! He was sure they were well. Something hopeful was growing inside him. He wasn't sure where it came from, but it was strong. He kept on walking until he came to the next village. Here, Makhosi saw changes in the land and vegetation. There was plenty of lush green grass for the animals to eat, and crops were growing tall in the fields.

Life here was very different from life in the village he had left behind. The setting sun threw a beautiful light over everything. Makhosi looked around and saw that the huts were very well cared for,

Makhosi and the Magic Horns

He chose one home and approached the entrance. A very rich-looking man stepped forward and looked him up and down.

"What do you want here and where do you come from? Do you think I will let you inside looking like that? Your clothes are filthy and you stink!" Makhosi looked at himself. He realized that the long journey had taken its toll. He went down to the river, took off his old clothes and had a good bath. Then he put the white bull's horns on the ground and knelt down, clapping his hands as he sang:

> *"Awe phondo lwami, olwasale mpini phondo lwami.*
> *Awe phondo lwami, awenze sigqoke phondo lwami!*
> *Oh, horns of mine, left to me in battle, horns of mine.*
> *Oh, horns of mine, make clothes so I can dress, horns of mine!"*

The magic worked once again. Right there in front of him he saw clothes made of the finest cloth. This new outfit was green, gold, dark red and sky blue, and had a matching hat with gold embroidery. There were even leather sandals, too. The old bag he was carrying was no more. In its place was a brand new leopard-skin one, big enough for the horns to fit inside. Makhosi's new clothes made him look like a prince.

Makhosi went to the entrance of the hut again. The same man stepped out, and he could not believe what he saw. Was his visitor a

29

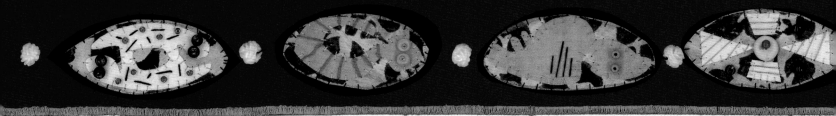

prince? He smiled broadly and said, "Please come in — you are welcome. It is not safe for you to walk alone at night. Come and sit inside." His attitude had completely changed. The two of them sat down and talked, man to man. A woman brought Makhosi a drink and everyone plied him with questions. Where had he come from? How far did he still have to go? Was he of noble birth?

Makhosi looked at these grasping, pretentious people, gave them the name of some imaginary place and said he was visiting a rich uncle. He kept quiet about his magic horns. His host offered him a very comfortable place to sleep for the night. In the morning, he woke up very early. He sang quietly to the horns to make lots of food and pots full of beer, so that his hosts would have plenty to share with their neighbors too, especially those less fortunate than themselves. The family was stunned by what they saw and pleaded with him to stay.

"Thank you, but I must go. It is very important that I continue to my uncle's home." And as soon as he had eaten, Makhosi went on his way.

The sun was high above him and his shadow was small under his feet when he finally came to his uncle's village. The people here looked happy and healthy. The children were running about playing with each other, and lots of families were down at the river. Everyone shouted with joy when they saw Makhosi approaching. His cousins and his aunt hugged and hugged him. Then his uncle appeared.

MAKHOSI AND THE MAGIC HORNS

"Hawu, Mshana, my nephew, is it really you, child of my sister?" he asked with a big smile on his face. They shook hands warmly.

Even though he had been safe all the way, the spirit of the white bull with him at all times, Makhosi was relieved to be there.

"Come inside, come inside!" First, Makhosi's uncle gave him a meal, and then asked about his sister and brother-in-law. Of course, the news was not good. "There is no time to waste!" cried his uncle after Makhosi had told him everything. "We must set out as soon as possible tomorrow, making sure to take those magic horns of yours with us."

They set out for Makhosi's home at the crack of dawn the next morning. For the journey Makhosi's uncle chose two of his strongest oxen, to which Makhosi then gave added power and speed using the magic horns. All day long they traveled on the backs of the oxen, stopping only to let the animals rest. They reached Makhosi's village just as night was falling.

The boy's parents were looking very weary and their smiles of greeting were tired ones, although thankfully they seemed no sicker than before. Makhosi's uncle put together all the herbs he needed for rainmaking, then he went up the hill and stood in the moonlight. He worked for a long time, with his nephew next to him, helping and learning.

By the time they had finished, heavy clouds had gathered and the next morning everyone woke up to the beautiful music of falling rain. Back at

Makhosi and the Magic Horns

home, Makhosi took out the white bull's horns and explained to his family what had happened along the way and what magic the horns had been able to perform. The boy sat down and clapped his hands. He began to sing his magic song. This time he asked the horns to perform their biggest, most important task — to heal the villagers and animals of their strange sickness. His uncle knelt down next to him, and together they sang and sang:

> *"Awe phondo lwami, olwasale mpini phondo lwami*
> *Awe phondo lwami, sicela impilo phondo lwami!*
> *Oh, horns of mine, left to me in battle, horns of mine.*
> *Oh, horns of mine, we ask for healing, horns of mine!"*

They did not stop singing until both Makhosi's parents had stood up from their beds, eyes wide open. The song grew and both parents joined in. More and more people were healed every hour. For days, the family took turns singing to the horns until every person and every beast was completely cured.

Only then did Makhosi take time to rest. And it was some time too before he sat with his family and friends to talk about his travels and his experiences along the way. "How you have grown!" they said, in the way that grownups always do. Although now they meant it in a different way, of course.

> *Cosi cosi iyaphela*
> *Here I rest my story.*

Lesotho

LESOTHO IS A small country surrounded totally by South Africa. It is known as the "Kingdom in the Sky" because almost 80 per cent of it lies 6,000 feet above sea level. The land is very mountainous. The two main mountain ranges are the Maluti and the Thaba Putsoa ("Blue Grey") mountains. The highest point in the Maluti range is Thabana Ntlenyana, which, despite its size, means "Nice Little Mountain."

Lesotho has a culture all its own. Its population is almost completely Basotho — the native people of this area — who live in villages high in the mountains. Basotho crafts include hand-woven wool and mohair tapestries, leather and sheepskin goods, and local pottery like the handmade clay pots Masilonyana discovers in this story. Woven reeds and grasses are important to the Basotho and the most well-known woven item is the traditional cone-shaped Basotho hat, or "mokorotlo," which has become the symbol of the country. The conical peak of Mount Qiloane is supposed to have inspired the hat's distinctive shape.

* The center for traditional arts and crafts in Lesotho is Teyateyaneng, named after the Teja-Tejane River that flows south of the village.

* Sotho is the national language of Lesotho as well as one of the eleven official languages of South Africa. Indeed, the word Lesotho means "the land of the people who speak Sotho."

* The annual Morija Arts and Cultural Festival is held every October in Morija, a small town just south of Maseru, Lesotho's capital city.

* Traditional Basotho blankets are used for more than keeping warm; they are a part of Lesotho's national dress. There are particular blankets for each stage of a person's life, and for special occasions.

* One of the highest waterfalls in southern Africa is in central Lesotho. At 624 feet, it is called Maletsunyane Falls, or "Place of Smoke."

* Ponies were introduced to Lesotho by Europeans in the mid-nineteenth century. They became very important to the Basotho because of their sturdiness and ability to endure the harsh terrain. People often ride them wearing a colorful Basotho blanket draped over one shoulder.

Masilo and Masilonyana

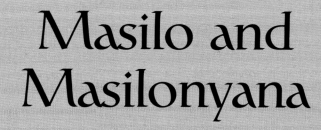

A LONG, LONG time ago, a poor family with two sons lived in a small village. The older son was called Masilo and the younger one Masilonyana. Life was not easy for the family. They worked very hard year after year, but their crops did not yield much food. Luckily, the boys were good hunters. From time to time, they went out to the mountains near their home to hunt for food. Their parents and their humble beginnings had taught them the importance of working together while hunting. "Be there for one another, no matter how hard the times," their mother and father advised.

One day, Masilo and Masilonyana went hunting with their dogs to a part of the country that they had never been to before. They looked around, not knowing what to expect.

"I think we should part here. You go this way and I will go that way with the dogs," said Masilo.

His younger brother nodded slowly and said, "Masilo, child of my father, I want you to know that

whatever happens here today, you can call on me and I will be there to help you." The older brother stepped forward, shook his hand and made the same promise. So they went their separate ways.

Masilo walked for a long time but found nothing. It was quiet in the forest, he thought. The only sounds came from his footsteps and the panting of the dogs trotting beside him.

Meanwhile, Masilonyana came across a small hill. He climbed up it and, to his great surprise, found three huge clay pots set upside down at the top.

"These are very well made and beautifully decorated pots," Masilonyana said to himself. "I wonder who put them here and why?" He walked around the three pots. They looked clean and fresh. It was clear that they had not been there for long.

"Hhm-m-mm. What could be underneath these clay pots in the middle of a forest?" Masilonyana wondered. He carefully pushed the first pot. Nothing happened. He pushed harder, but the pot would not budge. He tried the next one. That would not move either. By now, he was sweating and frustrated. He took a rest, then he tried the third pot. As soon as he touched it, he could hear odd noises coming from inside. How strange! Despite his fear, curiosity took hold and, with a gentle push from Masilonyana, the pot rolled over onto one side. Out crawled a strange old woman with long thick hair and long dirty fingernails. She was bent over and had to struggle to look up.

"You rude young man! Why did you disturb me from my sleep?" she scolded. Masilonyana was terrified, thinking she might be a witch. He called out to his older brother to come and help him.

Masilo, who was not far away, ran toward the hill. His hunting dogs went charging up ahead of him and attacked the old woman while Masilonyana clambered up a tree in terror. When Masilo reached the top of the hill, he hid behind some thick bushes to watch what would happen. Both boys shook with fear as they watched the dogs kill the old woman. Then, with absolute horror, the two brothers saw the old woman's long dirty fingernails suddenly grow and grow and grow! Out of the nails came a woman, then some children, and then all manner of animals: cattle, sheep, goats, chickens and ducks. They were small at first, but they grew bigger by the second, until all were life-size.

Masilonyana was so shocked by all this that his eyes looked as though they might pop out of his head.

"Thank you, Father," said the children, gazing up at Masilonyana as he sat in the tree. "You have freed us from that witch's spell!"

"You are my husband," said the woman. "These are our children, and the animals yours too." She smiled up at him as if she had

known him all her life. Masilonyana looked down at her and something deep inside him said, this is incredible; this is the most beautiful woman any man could ever wish to marry.

"I am very, very happy to agree to be your husband and the father of your children, our children. I am grateful, too, for all this wealth." So said Masilonyana, taking her hand in his, and looking in wonder at the children and animals. With all these cattle, he was now a rich man. He called to his brother again.

Masilo emerged from behind his bush and greeted everybody. He was smiling and congratulating everyone, but his heart was filled with jealousy. He wanted to take everything from his brother and be the one who went home rich, with such a beautiful wife and lovely children. He suddenly felt that he could not stand his brother anymore. He hated him! What had Masilonyana done to deserve such bounty? He decided not to show his feelings, however. "I must just pretend that everything is all right. But I will look for the right moment, and then I will get rid of him. I will kill him and take over everything." This was the dark plot that he hatched.

The group set off for the brothers' village. They walked for hours and it was hard to keep all those animals in line. The children were tired and, after a while, one of them said, "I am thirsty!" Everyone nodded. They knew the animals must be thirsty too.

40

MASILO AND MASILONYANA

"I think I know of a place that has a small spring somewhere near here," said Masilo. They stopped and sat down. The two brothers trooped off and found the spring. They took turns to fetch water for the mother and the children with the calabashes they had with them. Then they used a clay pot the woman had with her to give water to the animals. It was a long process, because each time one of the young men went to fetch the water, he had to go into a deep rocky hole and reach down to the cool pool below. When one brother was in the hole, the other one had to wait above to help him out again. It was very dangerous but they needed the water and Masilonyana trusted his older brother. He had no idea about any of the evil thoughts that were going on in Masilo's mind.

On their final trip to the spring, Masilo saw an opportunity to take all that his brother had recently gained. He picked up a big flat rock and closed the hole so Masilonyana could not climb out. He ran away from the cries of his brother and went quickly back to the woman and her children. When he reached the family, Masilonyana's new wife demanded to know where her husband was. Masilo said, "I am so sorry to tell you this, but my brother was swallowed by a huge animal in that hole where the spring was. He is dead. We must hurry and get back home before any more danger befalls us. You will be my wife now." As he shared this news, Masilo pretended to

41

be sad, but triumph soared inside him.

Back at the hole, poor Masilonyana cried and cried for help until his voice was hoarse. His brother did not return. Suddenly a big black snake that lived in the spring took pity on him.

"Are you a man or an animal?" asked the snake.

"I am a man," answered Masilonyana, not knowing whom he was talking to, for it was too dark to see anything. The snake came close and licked him all over with its thin black tongue. It opened its big mouth and swallowed him up whole. Then it slithered out of a hole it had made between the rocks and carried him home. It moved so fast that they arrived at the village that same night and went straight to the hut that the family used as a kitchen. The snake then wrapped itself up in a huge coil around the central fireplace with Masilonyana still hidden within.

Masilo had arrived earlier with all the livestock and the woman and children. Everyone was happy for him, but they were heartbroken to hear of Masilonyana's death.

In the morning, one of the children went into the kitchen for a drink of water. When she saw a big black snake with a huge stomach and black shiny eyes looking straight at her, she dropped the calabash and ran to tell her mother. They woke up everybody and the whole family went to see the extraordinary snake. Even the neighbors

and village elders came to look.

But before they could do anything, the snake began to speak:

"Masilo is an evil man,
His jealousy can poison the whole ocean.
He tried to kill his brother for his wealth.
But I saved Masilonyana, I brought him home.
He's right here in my belly."

And as he finished speaking, the big black snake spat out Masilonyana. He stood in front of his family and everyone looked at Masilo, shocked and disgusted by his behavior and his greed. At the same time, they rejoiced to see Masilonyana safe. His wife and children rushed to embrace him.

"How can we ever thank you?" the brothers' father asked the snake. "What would you like as a reward? Can we offer you a cow?"

The snake shook its head.

"May we offer you a goat?"

Again, the snake shook its head.

"Do you want to eat the evil brother?" asked one of the elders.

"Oh no, that would be terrible — he is poisonous!" said the snake, and it kept on looking at Masilonyana. His wife was worried that it might want to take him back to be its companion in the deep

waterhole. Then she had an idea. She ran to another hut and pulled a very beautiful, silky-smooth stone from her bag of belongings. The stone was called Tsilwana and was very special. Masilonyana's wife ran back to where everyone was and handed this stone to the snake.

"Thank you," said the snake. "This will look well in my home."

The snake was now happy to leave. As for Masilo, he was terrified to face the whole family and explain why he had done such an evil thing to his own brother. He took his few belongings and disappeared. He was never seen in that village again.

Masilonyana lived for many long years. He enjoyed being married to a loving woman and watching their children grow up, and, remembering his parents, he taught them that the most important values in life are humility and respect.

Cosi cosi iyaphela
Here I rest my story.

Swaziland

SWAZILAND IS ONE of the smallest countries on the African continent. Located in the southeast, most of the country is covered with grasses and small trees and bushes. Swaziland is landlocked, surrounded on three sides by South Africa, and bordered by Mozambique on its eastern border.

Hunting has always been a big part of Swazi life, just as it is a big part of Mbhekeni's life in this story. However, over the years, poaching, or illegal hunting, caused the near extinction of many animals, including the endangered black rhino. Today there are many national parks and reserves where wildlife is protected from poachers.

The baobab tree, like the one in the next story, is a familiar sight in the grassy savannah. It is a very big tree — growing up to 82 feet tall and 23 feet wide — and able to store up to 32,000 gallons of water inside its trunk, making it ideally suited to the dry conditions in which it grows. It is also sometimes known as the "upside-down tree" — maybe because its branches look like roots — based on a legend that it was planted upside down at the beginning of creation.

✳ If you drove along any road in Swaziland, you would see people dressed in colorful costume, including a vibrant, toga-like piece of clothing called the "mahiya." You might also meet Swazi warriors carrying shields, knob-sticks and sometimes spears and battle axes.

✳ Traditional ceremonies are very important in Swaziland. The most important is the sacred Ncwala or "Festival of the First Fruits," which takes place over three weeks in December.

✳ The Milwane Wildlife Sanctuary near Mbabane was the country's first conservation area. It is home to many animals, including zebras, giraffes, antelope, crocodiles, hippos and a variety of birds. The kudu, mentioned at the beginning of this story, is a type of antelope, and you might also see it roaming the Swazi savannah.

✳ A Swazi king does not appoint his heir. Swazi law states that "a king is king through his mother." When a king dies, the royal family decides which of his wives with a son of suitable age shall be the "Great Wife." The son of this "Great Wife," also known as the queen mother or "Great She-Elephant" will automatically become the next king.

✳ Cattle are the traditional symbol of wealth and prosperity. Marriage involves "lobola," a gift to the bride's parents, payable by the groom in the form of cattle. A similar system exists in most African societies.

The Great Hunter

IN THE VILLAGE of KwaManzi Mnyama there was no better hunter than Mbhekeni. He was respected by everyone. His wife and children were proud of him. People came from far and near to talk to him, to ask questions and to listen to the stories he told about his hunting expeditions. He wore the skins of some of the finest animals he had hunted, and their heads were arranged in front of his house like trophies.

"You see that set of horns over there — that kudu gave me such trouble before I could finally catch it. So I vividly remember that day whenever I look at those horns. The skin, too, was made into my most prized blanket." This is how Mbhekeni would talk about his adventures. Over the years, he became a role model to many young hunters.

"But don't you have days when you are faced with a dangerous animal and fear almost grabs your heart with hands of steel?" a youth asked him one day.

"Anyone who tells you that there are no days like that is a liar. I have had my share of times when I

48

thought I was face to face with death. So I silently sent messages of love and farewell to my wife and children. But then again I managed to survive, and made it safely home."

People listened to Mbhekeni's every word. The other men in the village admired all that he had done.

When their children had grown up and married, Mbhekeni and his wife were alone together for the first time in many years. They enjoyed their quiet life and looked forward to the birth of their grandchildren.

Then, one day, they realized they had no meat left in the house.

"Mbhekeni, dear father of my children. Can you please go out hunting so we can have some delicious meat for supper tonight?" asked his wife, with a warm smile.

"Of course I will. Let me prepare my bow and arrows and be sure I have everything I need."

When he was ready, Mbhekeni left the village and set out. He walked quickly but he made sure that he did not make any noise that might draw attention to him. His well-trained eyes were scanning his surroundings, this way and that way. He was searching for game, and also for dangers that might be lurking nearby.

Mbhekeni kept walking toward the open plains in the north, where he

knew animals would be grazing. He had been gone for only an hour or two when he spotted an impala. Its skin was shining and it looked noble and handsome; Mbhekeni was immediately taken by its beauty.

"I have hunted in these parts for years but I have never come across such a good-looking creature. This impala is very special!" he said to himself. Meanwhile the animal continued to graze peacefully. It seemed to be unaware of his presence and the danger he posed.

Mbhekeni aimed his arrow like the skilled hunter that he was, let it go and hit the impala in the chest. The beautiful creature was wounded but did not fall; it turned around and began to run leaving a trail of blood. Mbhekeni chased it and chased it until they came to a big baobab tree. The impala circled the tree and disappeared.

Mbhekeni followed the trail of blood to the tree, looked around and became very confused. The animal had simply vanished.

"This is strange!" he said to himself. "Am I losing my mind?"

In all his hunting days he had never seen or heard of anything like this. Had he been dreaming the whole thing? Tired and bewildered, he decided to sit down near the baobab tree and try to collect his thoughts…

Just then an old man suddenly appeared in front of him. Mbhekeni had not seen or heard him coming. How had he got there? Who could he be?

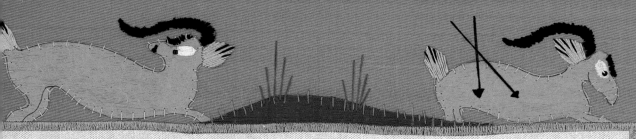

THE GREAT HUNTER

"You seem troubled," said the old man. "Are you looking for the impala you shot earlier?"

"Yes, I am. But how did you know that? Who are you and what do you want from me?" asked Mbhekeni, feeling very uneasy.

The old man simply smiled and said: "I think you should come with me. There is something that you need to see." He walked around the trunk of the baobab and led Mbhekeni to a hole in the trunk. Mbhekeni had walked around the same tree just a few minutes before and had seen nothing. How could this be? The old man did not even look back, he just climbed into the hole and Mbhekeni knew he had to follow.

The old man led Mbhekeni down some uneven steps inside the baobab tree. He moved with confidence, as if he knew the place well. There were many steps cut with great care inside the trunk of the tree and down past the roots. As they descended, Mbhekeni noticed that the lower ones were made with mud. They went down and down until they came to a village under the tree. The air was fresh and the place was flooded with a soft magic light. There were all kinds of birds and flowers, and fields of millet, sugarcane, and much more. Everything was growing beautifully. The houses were neatly decorated with gentle colors — golden brown, dark red, creamy white, soft gray. The patterns they created together were a joy to behold. This must be a really happy

place, thought Mbhekeni. He could not open his eyes wide enough as he walked in this strange community, following the old man who strode forward without speaking.

"What a lovely place, and what unusually handsome people!" he whispered to himself. Yet they were all looking so sad. Even the children who sat quietly in front of their homes had long faces and the women were crying pitifully.

"Where are we? And why is everyone so very sad?" he finally asked the old man, who was now leading him to a very big house where all the men were gathered together. They were talking in hushed voices and looking very gloomy too.

"Our prince is hurt. He was stabbed by an arrow in the chest. He almost did not make it down here alive," answered the old man.

The other men nodded their greetings to Mbhekeni and made space for him to sit with them.

"But this place looks so peaceful, why would one man hunt another?" asked Mbhekeni.

"Maybe you do not know much about us here," said one of the men. "All the people in this village can change themselves into animals when they go up the big sacred tree. When they get to the land above the tree, they can experience another life as an animal of their choice. And because our prince loves the impala, many young

men and women of our village have changed themselves into the same animal too so they can keep him company. But it is never safe. Lions and other hunters see these animals as easy prey."

"You see, our prince went out this morning and turned into an impala. He was grazing happily when a dreaded hunter from KwaManzi Mnyama village spotted him," added another man with tears in his eyes.

As the circle of men told Mbhekeni about their unusual way of life, the young prince lay nearby on a blanket, groaning painfully and clutching his chest. Then he opened his tired eyes and looked up. Mbhekeni felt as if he was looking straight through him. He wished he could disappear right there and then. He had never meant to cause these peace-loving people any pain. And now here he was listening with great anguish as they talked about the many times a horrible hunter from KwaManzi Mnyama village had come and killed their young men and women.

"I am the terrible hunter," he confessed. "I am so very sorry, really I am! But from today your people will never have to fear me again." He stood up to go. The old man did not accompany him this time. Mbhekeni's eyes were filled with tears as he rushed back to the steps leading into the baobab tree. He climbed up them as fast as he could. When he finally reached the entrance to the tree and could breathe the air outside and feel the sun's rays on his skin, he fell down and cried hard for the people of the village. He cried for their beloved prince, too. How could he change and not be the hunter they so feared and hated?

Then he heard a big thud next to him. It was the same impala that he had shot earlier, and it was dead. He knew at once that the prince was also dead. He could almost hear the wailing and crying of the women and children down in the village below the baobab tree.

Mbhekeni looked for something he could use to dig a hole. He cut a strong stick from a tree nearby and started digging. It took a long time and it was hard work. But he told himself that he was doing this for the prince and his people. He knew that the impala had been returned to him so that he could make amends for all the wrong he had done to them over the years. He removed the impala's skin with great care, folded it and put it aside. Then he buried the animal like a good friend. He marked the place with a rock in case he came near that place again.

By the time he had walked all the way back to the KwaManzi Mnyama village, Mbhekeni was a changed man. His wife saw him coming and stood at the gate to greet him. Then she noticed that he did not look happy. "Mbhekeni, where is the meat, why are you coming home with only the skin of the animal?" she asked.

THE GREAT HUNTER

Mbhekeni did not answer. He looked so very tired. She made him something to drink and let him sit quietly for a while. She brought him a delicious pumpkin dish she had prepared earlier. He ate in silence. Then he took the impala skin outside to spread it on a big flat rock he always used to dry out the skins he brought back from his many hunting trips. And after that, with a heavy heart, he told his wife everything that had happened to him that day.

She listened to him until he had finished. She tried to imagine what he had told her, but it was hard. How could such a village exist under a baobab tree? This was very strange news to her and to many of their friends who came to visit the following day.

"I have decided never to go hunting again. This is the end of my hunting days," said Mbhekeni. No one could believe it. How could this happen to the most respected hunter in the land? But Mbhekeni kept his word. He continued to tell people the stories of his hunting days, only now he reminded them that they should take care — any impala could be a young man or woman from the village under the sacred tree. Ever since then, the impala has been regarded with special respect by the people of Swaziland.

Cosi cosi iyaphela
Here I rest my story.

57

Senegal

SENEGAL IS IN West Africa, with the Atlantic Coast on one side and otherwise bordered by Mauritania in the north, Mali in the east, and Guinea and Guinea-Bissau in the south. It is made up of three sections, divided by its three major rivers. The Senegal River forms the country's northern border, the Gambia River cuts through the center of the country, and the Casamance River flows through the south. The rivers all flow from east to west.

Most of the people of Senegal live along the coast, and the majority of that population is Wolof, the native people of Senegal. Dakar, the capital city, and Senegal's other major cities are all located in the west. In fact, Dakar is situated on the Cap-Vert peninsula, the westernmost tip of Africa. Fishing is the second most common occupation, after farming, and there are many fishing villages along the coast of Senegal. Fishing is mostly done from a "pirogue," a small but long Senegalese boat carved out of wood and sometimes fitted with a sail, like old Abbege's boat in this story. Many people depend on the waters of Senegal, just as the fishermen in this next story depend on Sea Wind.

❋ Legend says that the name Senegal came from the Wolof name for a dugout canoe ("sunu gaal"), which was mispronounced by Portuguese sailors in the mid-fifteenth century.

❋ The Wolof are an ethnic group found in Senegal; they represent about 40 per cent of the total population.

❋ Fish is the main source of protein for the Senegalese, and they are among the biggest fish eaters in the world.

❋ Fish that live in the waters off Senegal include barracuda, cobia, tarpon, stingray, ombrine and carranque.

❋ Lake Retba, north east of Dakar, is known as the Pink Lake because of its color. It is very salty, like the Dead Sea, and the minerals turn the water pink when the sunlight hits it. This happens most noticeably during the dry season.

❋ One of the most important bird sanctuaries in the world is in Senegal. Over three million migrating birds stop at the Djoudj National Park because it is one of the first places with permanent water south of the Sahara. Almost four hundred species of birds visit the park, the majority of which are pelicans and flamingos.

Sea Wind

ALL DAY LONG, Sea Wind roams over islands and seas, through forests and plains, driving herds of timid deer toward the waterholes. In all the daylight hours, he refreshes plants, uplifts birds and heralds the changing seasons.

Yet of an evening, when he is tired, he folds his wings and sinks down as the red sun sets. He floats below the clouds, hovers for a moment as he chooses a sand dune or a quiet glade, then settles down to rest.

The great bushland knows his secrets; she knows that each night he takes the form of bird or beast so as to slumber undisturbed.

"Hush, Sea Wind is sleeping," she murmurs.

The green parrot on the wing — that is Sea Wind. The silver lizard on the moonlit hill — that is him. Over the Great Lake you may see a flight of pink flamingos on the pale horizon — that is Sea Wind, too. Sometimes he rests close by a village. Then he stretches out tall and handsome, a warrior lying on the grass, slumbering, head cradled on one arm.

One time when Aminata, a maid of Maca, went to fetch fresh water, she found Sea Wind sleeping

beneath a tree and she stopped to look at him. She took him for a wayfarer, a stranger from another land. But what a man: the hero of her dreams, the man she had sought since love first stirred in her chest.

Dust mingled with sweat upon his forehead, his body was scarred with scratches and weeping cuts. With gentle, timid hands, the girl cleaned his wounds and bathed his face and eyes.

It was a still, starlit night for the meeting of Aminata and the copper-colored stranger. She was so full of love she did not hear the old fisherman Abbege poling his way back from Gorom, grumbling as he staggered up the path, bent double beneath his bundle of nets and lines.

The old man used to listen out for Sea Wind and talk to him. "Frish, Frish," he would call.

Out of a tree dived a toucan at dawn's first light. The parrot's eyes flushed pink, and the guinea fowl stretched its neck and rushed off in search of seeds. There came a rustling as all the animals awoke. With a deep sigh, the broad expanse of open country awoke. Sea Wind opened his eyes. He saw above him a maiden's face with such a tender look.

"What is your name?" he asked.

"Aminata," the girl replied.

"And who was the first boy to tell you how pretty you are?"

She blushed.

"You do not reply, Aminata."

61

"I like to hear you speak my name," she sighed.

"It is as fresh as the water in your jug," he said.

She lowered her eyes and held out the pitcher for him to drink. He took a long swallow.

"I have long awaited a stranger beneath this tree," she murmured. "A man such as you."

He was silent, and then gently he said, "Aminata, in my wanderings I too have dreamed. My dream was of a daughter of the People's tribe who was just like you. But I am a traveler, I never halt; I am from here and there and everywhere where I am not. Yet somehow I long to stay with you. I grow tired of rushing to and fro about the world."

Before their huts, the women pounded millet with their pestles. Abbege unhooked his nets and set off toward the river once again. As he passed by the couple, he was muttering to himself, "Sea Wind is growing old and deaf; he does not hear me."

When he reached the end of the path, they heard him calling — "Frish, Frish" — as he unfurled his patched white sail. Then, all at once, the stranger rose, as light as a butterfly's wing, and gazed into the girl's deep brown eyes, as if making a promise to her.

"Frish is my name," he said softly.

Then, a deep-throated laugh burst from him and his white teeth flashed.

62

Sea Wind

"Well, I must accompany the fisherman to Gorom. He calls my name and I must push him upstream. He thinks I am old and deaf. Oh no, Aminata — Sea Wind is neither old nor deaf; he has the swiftest feet and the sharpest ears."

She did not dare ask when he would return. But he read the unasked question in her eyes.

"I shall return, Aminata. I'll be here this evening beneath the tree."

All day long, her thoughts dwelt on the meeting. When evening came, she was there, waiting by the tree.

With the first trembling touch of night he came to her, bending the grass and raising a puff of dust to tickle the housedogs' noses as they sat before the huts, biting and scratching their mangy coats.

Aminata took him home to her family and when her father returned from hunting, they all sat down to eat, Sea Wind eating with his fingers like a man and drinking beer as he related his adventures. By and by, the elders came to listen to him as he spoke. Voices murmured long into the night in Aminata's hut, for Sea Wind had chosen her to be his wife.

In the passing of the years, Sea Wind and Aminata had two fine children. The first was a boy, Mamadu Marta, which means Sea Breeze; the second was a girl, Binetu, which means Flower Wind.

Never were children so lively. In the meadows where the washerwomen spread their linen on the grass to dry, they would

rush about until they were quite out of breath; each time they passed, they made the clothes swing to and fro.

They would wander into the forest, blowing with all their might into the bushes, putting to flight the partridge and leading deer astray with their mischievous gusts of wind.

Mamadu Marta would accompany old Abbege to the fishing grounds where the old fisherwoman would cry, "Frish, Frish."

And Mamadu Marta would come rushing over the waves, leaping into the stern of the pirogue and blowing the sail fit to tear the canvas. Binetu learned singing from birds and crickets, and would warble for hours as she walked through fields of flowers, gathering golden sunbeams and scattering them to the breeze. Her breath was fragrant with lilies and orange-blossom. Aminata's garden was full of pretty flowers that her daughter brought from far and near, helping them to flourish with her songs. Her father called the songs "Flowers of the Wind."

It was not often that journeys brought Sea Wind to the village but, when he came, he would stay there for a while. Then Aminata was so happy. He would spend whole nights with her and tell the little ones stories from the lands of the Crimson Sunset.

Throughout those long nights, boats were becalmed upon the sea, and an eerie silence reigned across the world. The earth, water and

SEA WIND

grass all found it hard to bear — but no one was troubled at Maca, where it seemed a short pause before Sea Wind told another story to his children and blew gently upon the embers of the hearth.

For a few years, Sea Wind returned at every change of season. Then, when Aminata gave birth to her third child, he did not come at all. Aminata was mortally ill after the birth. Her third child was the most handsome of all, with soft black eyes and laughter that was warm and caressing like a summer's breeze. Aminata held him to her breast till her last breath, talking to him as if he understood, hoping for a miracle that would bring back her husband.

Old Abbege said later that, toward the dawn, he saw a big white seagull pass low over the water, issuing a heart-rending cry and heading for the village. When Abbege went into the village and pushed open Aminata's door, he swore he saw the seagull standing on one leg and gazing at the mother and child.

And as he watched the woman and the bird, he heard Aminata say, "You have returned at last, proud nomad of my dreams. Now that you are here, I grieve no more. Farewell, fond Frish — I love you dearly."

The white seagull circled for some moments above the village, then turned and flew straight out to sea again.

Sea Wind's third child grew up a sturdy boy. His childhood was that of a normal boy, save that he did not play with other children of his age. He preferred to wander by himself, befriending baby birds who had fallen from their nests. He was gentle, peace-loving and kind. The villagers called him Alama, which means Breath of Mercy.

One day, Sea Breeze, Flower Wind and Breath of Mercy all flew away from their village home.

To Sea Breeze, his father gave the realm of oceans, waves, rivers and swamps. Abbege's sons whistle for him.

The girl, Flower Wind, haunts the fields and woods, and everywhere she goes she brings warm days in spring, ripe fruit in autumn, and on hot days, when the air shimmers in the sun, it is she who tosses up those little glittering grains of gold that are neither insect nor flower.

Alama, the last-born, has the most beautiful realm of all. He rocks and comforts the sad people of the world; he sings for those who mourn, he brings a breath of joy and a soothing caress to comfort the sick and the poor.

Cosi cosi iyaphela
Here I rest my story.

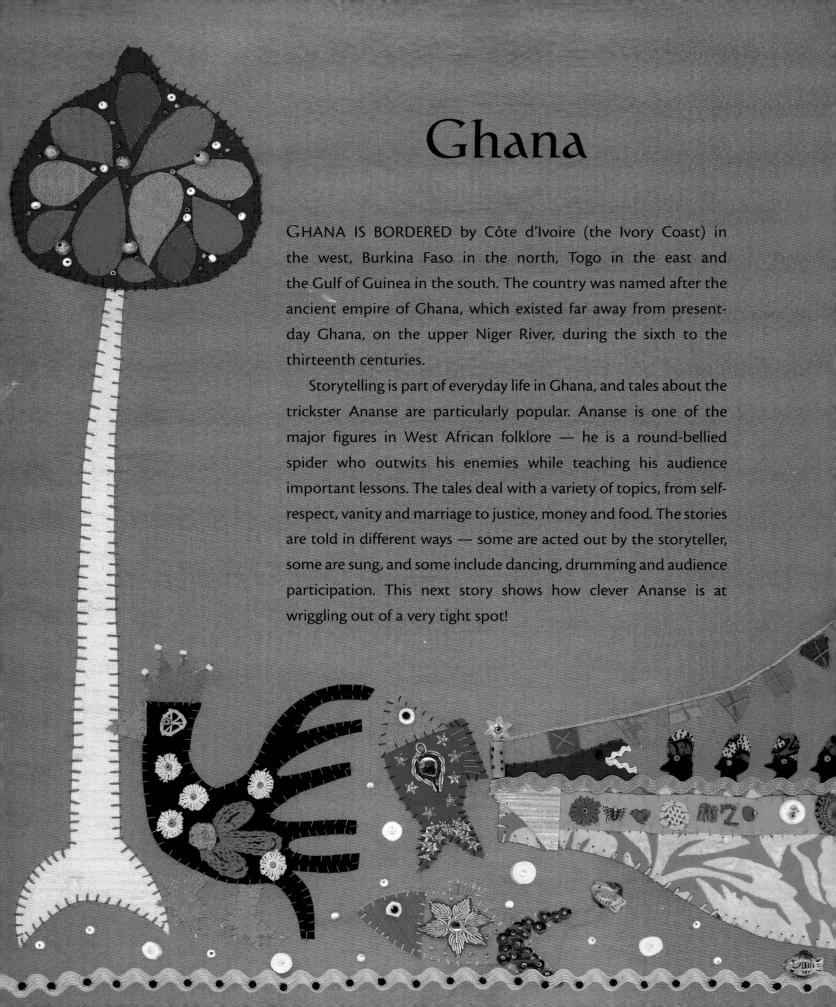

Ghana

GHANA IS BORDERED by Côte d'Ivoire (the Ivory Coast) in the west, Burkina Faso in the north, Togo in the east and the Gulf of Guinea in the south. The country was named after the ancient empire of Ghana, which existed far away from present-day Ghana, on the upper Niger River, during the sixth to the thirteenth centuries.

Storytelling is part of everyday life in Ghana, and tales about the trickster Ananse are particularly popular. Ananse is one of the major figures in West African folklore — he is a round-bellied spider who outwits his enemies while teaching his audience important lessons. The tales deal with a variety of topics, from self-respect, vanity and marriage to justice, money and food. The stories are told in different ways — some are acted out by the storyteller, some are sung, and some include dancing, drumming and audience participation. This next story shows how clever Ananse is at wriggling out of a very tight spot!

* Ghana means "Warrior King" and was the title of rulers of the ancient empire, which was actually called Wagadugu.

* Traditionally, the elders of Ghana pass down knowledge through stories, often drawn from real life past and present, and often with a religious or moral message. The Ananse stories are part of this tradition.

* It was the Akans of Ghana who first told Ananse stories, which they called "Anansesem" (literally, "The Spider Story") and which then spread throughout West Africa. From there the stories became popular in many countries around the world.

* In the 1950s and 1960s, many of the oral stories of Ghana were written down so that they could be used in schools. Ananse stories are now a part of what every child learns at school in Ghana.

* African talking drums, or "dondos" as they are called in Ghana, mimic the sounds of speech and are used by "griots," West African storytellers. Dondos are shaped like an hourglass and have strings that control the sound.

Ananse and
the Impossible Quest

ONE DAY, THE KING, who thought himself very wise and powerful, decided he was growing tired of Kwaku Ananse, the spider man. He thought Ananse was getting rather bigheaded and a bit too clever for his own good. No matter how difficult the tasks he set for him, Ananse always managed to find an answer. Something had to be done about it. The king thought long and hard, and then had an idea.

He summoned Ananse to the palace and told him he'd been chosen for a very special quest: "There are two very precious things that I wish to have, and I've chosen you, Kwaku Ananse, to get them for me."

"Yes?" said Ananse eagerly, excited about the thought of a new challenge. "What are they?"

"If I should tell you," the king replied with a sly smile, "I'm sure it would be far too easy for you. So to make it a little more of a challenge for your great wisdom, I am not prepared to reveal what the objects are — only that I want them. If you bring

them to me within a week, I will see that you are very well rewarded with land and honor. But, if you fail me, you will die."

Kwaku Ananse was deep in thought as he made his way home, but walking through the forest he saw the birds flying around and that gave him an idea. He stopped and called all the birds to him.

"I'm on a special mission for the king," he said. "I have always been a good friend to you and all I want now is a small token of your friendship in return. Fly by my house and each of you leave just one feather. Now off you go, and don't forget."

When Ananse arrived home, he found his wife and son staring at an enormous heap of feathers.

"Don't just stand there!" he said. "Stick the feathers all over me as quickly as you can and make me into a bird."

In no time at all, he was covered in feathers of all shapes, sizes and colors. He looked like the strangest bird you could ever imagine. His two thin arms were transformed into wings and as he flapped them, he began to fly, higher and higher, until he could see the king's palace in the distance.

He flew into the royal courtyard and saw the king with some of his elders sitting in the shade of a great tree, so he perched on a high branch where he could hear all that was said.

GHANA

"What's that strange bird?" asked the king.

"Send for Ananse," suggested one of the elders. "He's sure to know."

"I'm pleased to say that I cannot do that," replied the king, and he explained the impossible quest he had set Ananse.

"What a clever idea," said the elders, "and what is it you want him to get for you?"

"He must go to Death's house and get me his golden slippers and his golden broom. Nobody goes to visit Death and returns, so even if he knew what I wanted, we would still be finished with him. This way I can put an end to him whatever happens."

Ananse flew away to the sound of their laughter. When he reached home, his wife helped him to unstick his feathers and prepared some food for the journey, and then he set out on his quest.

Ananse had been walking for a few hours when he came to a fast-flowing river. As he looked for a way across, he realized that he was feeling hungry. He was just about to tuck in when, to his amazement, he heard the gurgling voice of the rushing water, asking for a share.

"You never know when you might want a friend," Ananse said to himself. He threw half of his food into the torrent, which slowed a little to reveal a line of stepping stones leading across to the other side. As soon as he had eaten his fill, Ananse crossed the river safely.

ANANSE AND THE IMPOSSIBLE QUEST

Soon he came to the great, gray house where Death lived. He banged on the door and was welcomed inside by an old man. Death didn't have many casual visitors and so he was particularly pleased to see this one.

"Why not stay the night?" Death asked slyly, after Ananse had introduced himself.

"How very kind of you," said Ananse, knowing full well that if he was silly enough to go to sleep in Death's house, he wouldn't wake up in the morning.

The guest room was dark and dusty, but in the middle of it was a huge bed with a soft feather mattress and warm, cozy covers.

Ananse got into the bed and was lying there, pinching himself to stay awake, when he heard the door open.

"Not asleep yet?" Death asked.

"I'm afraid not," said Ananse. "I can never get to sleep without a pair of golden slippers on my feet. I don't suppose you've got any?"

"Well, as it happens, I have," replied Death. "I'll go and get them."

So Death brought Ananse the golden slippers.

Don't ask me how Ananse managed to get through the night without falling asleep, but as morning light crept through the window, he was still wide awake and went down to breakfast clutching the golden slippers.

Death was sitting on the porch in a very grumpy mood, which wasn't improved by an irritating fly buzzing around his head.

"I'll get it," Ananse said, and he picked up the golden broom, which just happened to be leaning against the wall.

Before Death could say anything, Ananse was running around swinging at the fly and catching Death with a few hearty smacks in the process. Then, grasping the slippers in one hand and the broom in the other, Ananse chased the fly off the porch and around the corner. Once he was out of sight, he took to his heels and ran just as fast as his legs would carry him, away from Death's house.

It took Death a while to realize he'd been tricked, but then he set off after Ananse, as swift as the wind.

Ananse could hear Death just behind him when suddenly he found himself splashing about in water and he knew he was in the river that he had crossed the day before.

"Please, please!" he said. "Remember the delicious food I gave you on my way here? Well, I need your help now. Death is behind me and he'll soon catch up unless you grow into a flood and slow him down."

Quick as a flash, the river became a great deep lake that spread toward Death and stopped him in his tracks. Ananse didn't stop running until he reached home, and then it was only to put the slippers and broom in a bag before setting off for the palace.

GHANA

The king was in his favorite place under the tree in the courtyard, sheltering from the sweltering sun. He saw Ananse approaching with a bag that just might contain what he'd sent him for…but how could that be?

"I'm not sure that I've got what you wanted. Could you just tell me what it was?" Ananse was enjoying himself.

With his elders all around him, the king had no choice but to reply that what he wanted was Death's golden slippers and golden broom. You should have seen his face when Ananse took those very items from the bag! The king was hopping mad, but he had to keep his word and Ananse was given land and honor as his reward.

As Ananse was leaving, the king suddenly remembered the strange bird he had seen, and asked if he knew what it was. Ananse thought for a while. Ever ready with a clever reply, he had the sense this time to realize that sometimes it is wiser to appear ignorant. So he kept the secret, and I hope you will too.

Cosi cosi iyaphela
Here I rest my story.

Sudan

SUDAN IS THE largest country in Africa and the tenth largest in the world. It is located in the northeastern part of the continent, bordered by the Red Sea and by many countries including Ethiopia to the east, Egypt in the north, Chad in the west, and Uganda and the Congo in the south.

Sudan gained independence in 1956, the people holding elections to establish their own government. In this story, set many years ago, the sultan is the ruler of the country and when he dies, his son Jalal takes over from him. Today, Sudan has a president who is elected by the people.

The Nile River, the longest river in the world, flows throughout the whole length of Sudan, from south to north. As in the neighboring country of Egypt, the river is a very important part of life for the people and animals living near it, being a major source of water and other resources.

* Sudan is one of the most diverse countries in the world. There are over six hundred different ethnic groups and over four hundred different languages are spoken.

* Sudan is an agricultural country, which means that most people work on the land, growing crops and tending animals, instead of working in factories or offices.

* Most people in Sudan live in small towns and villages, although some live as nomads, traveling through the desert with their herds of sheep and camels. There are a few big cities, but only about a third of the population lives there.

* The Sudanese people dress in clothing typical of the Middle East. Many of the men wear an ankle-long white gown called a "galabiya," while the women wear a colorful long garment known as a "thobe."

* Nubia, an area within the Nile valley, is the site of over two hundred ancient pyramids. Several of these were built for the warrior queens of two ancient Sudanese tribes — Napata and Meroë.

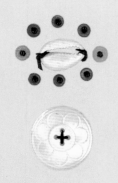

The Story of the Wise Mother

ONCE UPON A TIME, there lived a sultan and his wife. They had only one son. He was called Jalal and his parents were very proud of him. Jalal was clever, courageous and strong, as well as generous like his father. He grew into a kind young man who was loved by everyone.

One day, the sultan fell ill. Jalal did not rest trying to find a cure for his father's illness. He brought many baseers, learned medicine men, who tried many cures. But not one of them could help the old man. Every day the illness worsened until one morning the sultan passed away. All the people were sad at the loss of their just leader.

His son, Jalal, became the new sultan in his place. Jalal's mother loved her only son very much. She knew that he was well liked yet she worried about his safety and so tried to guide him whenever she could. Indeed Jalal's mother was a very wise woman, much respected by the people of the land. One day she said to him, "Oh son, take care!

And beware of so-called friends! Most of them will only be looking for your money, so you must choose your friends cautiously and wisely."

The young sultan was astonished. "But how can I do that, mother?" Jalal asked. His mother told him to choose a friend and see what happened. He chose one of the merchants' sons. They spent quite a bit of time together. It looked like their friendship was really growing.

Jalal's mother then asked him to invite his friend for breakfast. Jalal did so. The young man came to the palace. He was given something to drink and the two friends sat and talked. Often they stole glances at the door, wondering why the servants were taking so long. Both young men were very hungry. But the sultan's mother delayed the meal until noon. Then she sent them the food. It consisted of only three eggs, nothing else. The young men were puzzled by this, but they asked no questions.

The friend took one egg. The young sultan took another one. Each ate his egg. Then the friend took the third egg and gave it to Jalal. The young sultan ate it, and the friend went home. Jalal then went to his mother, who asked him what had happened. When he told her, she advised him not to befriend this young man. She said, "He is a bad person, trying to deceive you into believing that he likes you more than himself. He will take your money." So he left that friend and chose another one.

This new friend was the son of the head of the guards. They soon became the closest of companions.

Again, the mother asked her son to invite his friend for breakfast. The friend came. As before, she delayed the meal until noon. Both of them sat patiently although they were very hungry. Three eggs were brought. The friend ate one and Jalal ate one. Then the friend ate the third one and went away. The sultan went to his mother, who asked him about what had happened. He told her.

The mother advised him not to continue being friends with this man, because he was clearly very selfish and if he ever found a chance, he would take Jalal's money. She told him to choose a third friend. This time it was not easy, and he was wondering what his mother was really looking for. He looked here and he looked there, but couldn't find anyone.

One day, while he was wandering in the forest, he came across the home of a poor woodcutter and his son, who was Jalal's age. Jalal greeted them and they invited him to sit and eat with them. They gave him simple food and some water in a very old pot. He really enjoyed their company. The woodcutter's son, who was called Khalid, told Jalal many stories and showed him some tricks. Khalid showed him around the forest and taught him some of the skills of the forester. All the while, they were talking and found a lot to laugh about, too.

THE STORY OF THE WISE MOTHER

The sultan felt great pleasure and happiness, unlike any he had felt before. He went home and did not say anything to his mother about the woodcutter and his son. But he thought about them all the time. He began to visit his new friends regularly. Each time he learned more about life, its difficulties and how to solve those difficulties. He still had not told them who he really was. So the friendship was easy and they felt like any two young people getting to know one another. Then one day, the woodcutter's son learned that the young man was in fact the sultan. Khalid said that he was not suited to be Jalal's friend. But the sultan insisted: "There is no good reason why we cannot continue being friends. You and I are more alike than anyone else I have ever met."

So Jalal and Khalid continued to be friends. Often, when Jalal went back to his mother, he was covered in dirt or had a cut on his cheek. At other times there were wounds on his knees and cuts on his face and arms. His mother saw all this and kept quiet. She noticed too that Jalal was very happy whenever he came back from the forest. For some time they went on like this. Then one day the mother asked her son, "So tell me. What is your new friend's name?"

"Khalid, and I like him a lot," said Jalal. And he went on to tell his mother of the many good times they had had and what a wise young man his friend was.

THE STORY OF THE WISE MOTHER

"Then let us invite this Khalid for breakfast," said his mother. This time Jalal was much more anxious; he wondered if he was going to have to give this friend up too. And his friend was very nervous about coming to the palace.

It was a bright sunny day. The birds sang sweetly up in the sky. Khalid was welcomed and he sat quietly with his friend. The same thing happened as before. The mother took her time. The three eggs were brought to the two young men very late, and they were both hungry. Each one took an egg and ate it. The third egg was left uneaten. Khalid took the third egg, cut it with his knife, and divided it into two. He gave the sultan one half and he took the other.

After that, the woodcutter's son went home. The mother asked her son, the sultan, how the meal had gone. He told her.

Then she said to him, "This is a true friend. Stay true to him yourself, although he is poor." Jalal followed his mother's advice. He and his mother were sure that Khalid was a good, honest, wise young man. In time, Jalal appointed him prime minister of the sultanate.

They remained good friends ever after.

Cosi cosi iyaphela
Here I rest my story.

Ethiopia

ETHIOPIA IS A large country located in the "Horn of Africa," a section of land that sticks out for hundreds of miles from the main body of the continent. With over seventy million people, Ethiopia is one of the most highly populated countries in Africa and has a very rich culture and history.

Ethiopia is bordered by Eritrea to the north, Djibouti to the northeast, Kenya to the south, Sudan to the west and Somalia to the east. It is the site of about 80 per cent of Africa's tallest mountains. Formerly, the culture of Ethiopia experienced very little outside influence, mainly because of its mountains — outsiders could not pass over them, so Ethiopians developed their own traditions. Since then, Ethiopia has evolved into a modern country, where old traditions exist alongside new developments, as you will see in this next story.

Food is a very important part of Ethiopian culture. It is a sign of respect to share a meal with someone, just as the king shares his with the merchant in this story.

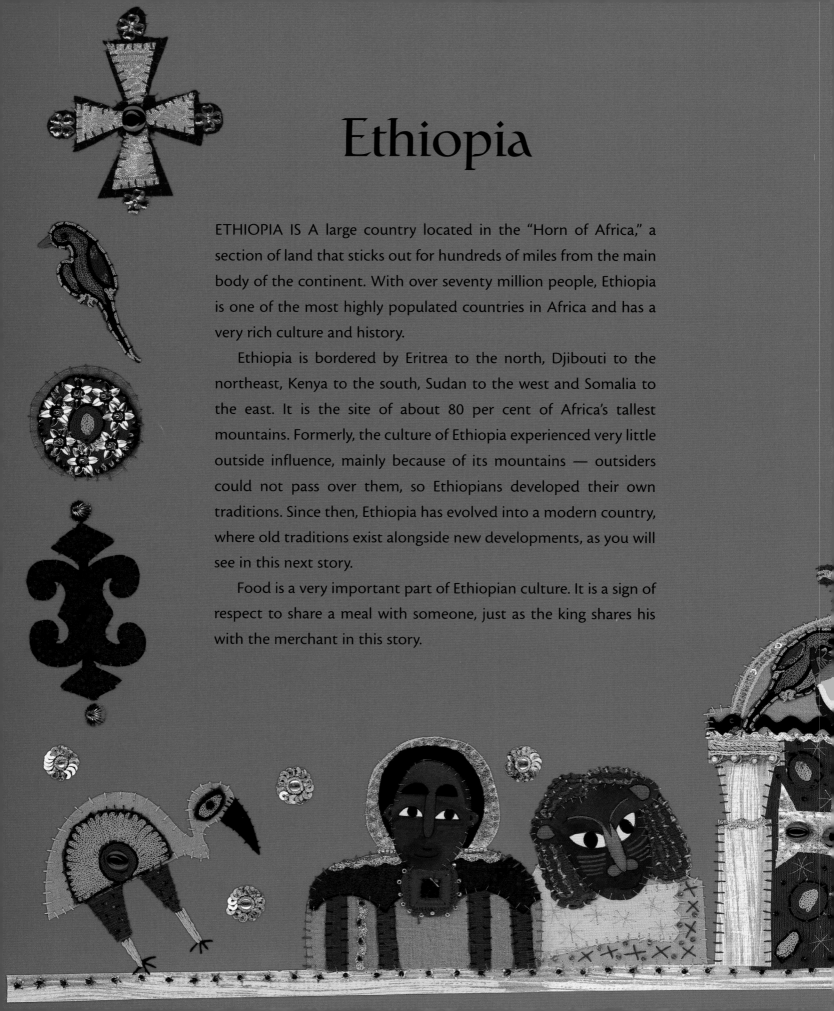

* Ethiopia was the only African country not to be colonized. It was also one of the first countries in the world to adopt Christianity.

* Ethiopia is known as the "cradle of humanity" because some of the oldest human fossils on the planet have been found there. Some are as old as 5.8 million years!

* Amharic is the official language of Ethiopia. English, French, Italian and Arabic are also widely spoken.

* As in all African countries, food is not eaten with knives and forks in Ethiopia. Instead, people use "injera" — a type of large flatbread made with sourdough — to scoop up their food.

* Ethiopia is the second biggest maize producer in Africa, and agriculture is the foundation of the country's economy. Ethiopia's other main crops include coffee, pulses, cereals and sugarcane.

* A typical Ethiopian breakfast dish is "firfir" or "fitfit." It is made from shredded injera with spices. "Dulet," a spicy mixture of tripe, liver, beef, and peppers with injera is also a popular way to start the day.

Everything Changes, Everything Passes

ONCE THERE WAS a merchant who traveled far and wide through all the land of Ethiopia, selling his wares. One day, as he was going along the road, he saw a crowd of people.

"What are they doing?" he thought. "What are they looking at?" And he hurried over to join them.

The people were watching a farmer who was plowing his field. Yoked to the plow in place of an ox there was a man. The farmer was whipping him cruelly.

"Go on, go on, you lazy good for nothing," he was shouting. "Pull harder!"

The man yoked to the plow pulled with all his might. Sweat was running down his tired back, but the farmer did not think he was working hard enough. The merchant was saddened by this pitiful sight, and tears began to fall from his eyes. The man looked up and saw his distress.

"Don't cry for me," he said. "Don't stop your journey on my account."

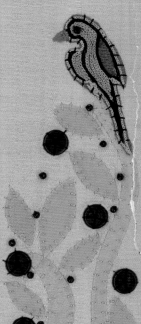

88

The merchant was impressed by the man's courage and dignity.

"This is wrong; this is cruel," he said, "that one man should put another man under a yoke as if he was an ox."

But the man said, "Listen, my friend. Everything changes, everything passes, and my suffering will pass too."

So the merchant, shaking his head sadly, went on his way.

A few years later, his travels took him to the very same place again, and he remembered the strange sight he'd seen before.

He stopped a passerby and said to her, "A few years ago, in this very place, I saw a man pulling a plow like an ox. What's happened to him? Can he still be alive?"

The woman laughed.

"He is," she said. "He didn't die. God looked down on him and took pity on his misery. He gave him riches and honor and that very same man is now the king of the whole region."

The merchant could hardly believe his ears.

"What?" he said. "In such a short time he has risen from being a slave to being a king?"

"Yes," the woman said. "If you don't believe me, go and see him for yourself."

89

So the merchant hurried to the king's palace and slipped in through the gate. The man he remembered, now dressed in fine new clothes instead of old rags, was sitting in state, surrounded by crowds of people. The merchant was so happy for him he laughed out loud.

The king heard him laugh and called out to him, "Who are you, stranger? Why are you laughing?"

"Well, sir," the merchant said, "as I traveled through this place a few years ago, I saw you pulling a plow like an ox and I wept for you. I was on the same road today and I heard that you had become king so I came here to see you with my own eyes and to rejoice in your good fortune."

The king smiled.

"Come," he said, "and sit beside me. Let's eat and drink," and he shared his meal with the merchant and gave him gifts as well.

When they had finished eating, the king said, "My son, God will bless you for remembering the poor man under the yoke."

"How could I forget you!" the merchant cried. "And to see you now like this! It's marvelous! Wonderful!"

"Yes," said the king, "but everything changes, everything passes, and this good fortune of mine will pass too."

The merchant went on his way, but when a few more years had passed, he returned once more, and hurried straight to the palace of the king to see how his friend was faring. He ran in through the gates, but there, seated in state, was another king, a man he had never seen before.

"Who is this?" he said to the people around him. "What happened to the previous king?"

"The old king died," they told him. "This man is king now."

The merchant bowed his head and wept.

"Show me his grave," he said, "so that I can pay him my respects."

So the people took him to the graveyard and showed him the stone under which the old king was buried. Sweet grasses blew in the wind and trees shaded his grave. Words were carved on the tombstone and the merchant spelled them out. "Everything changes, everything passes," he read, "and even this will pass too."

With a heavy heart, the merchant went on his way.

Many years later, the merchant, who was much older now, passed the same way again. He was very eager to visit the graveyard and hurried to it. Whatever else has happened, the king's grave will still be here, he thought. That cannot change. That cannot pass.

But a modern city had grown up in the meantime and the graveyard had disappeared. The grass, the shady trees and the tombstones had all vanished. Workers were carrying bricks and

panes of glass and trucks were spilling out tons of sand and cement.

The merchant called to a worker and said, "Please, my friend, there was a graveyard here once, and on one of the headstones there was an inscription which read, 'Everything changes, everything passes, and even this will pass too.' Do you know where it has gone?"

"I remember that headstone," the man said, "but you won't find it now. The city's master plan has swept the graveyard and all the headstones away, and in its place is that great building. Look."

The merchant looked to where the man was pointing and saw a sleek modern building with gleaming windows stretching up into the sky. He shook his head.

"My friend was right," he said. "Everything changes, everything passes, and one day even this great building will disappear, too."

Cosi cosi iyaphela
Here I rest my story.

Sources

Africa

◆ "African Voices," Smithsonian National Museum of Natural History, http://www.mnh.si.edu/africanvoices/ (accessed 22 November 2005)

◆ Davies, Stephen, "Songs of our Fathers," *Africa Geographic* (Summer 2007)

◆ MacDonald, K. C., "Griot: African Storytelling Tradition," PBS, http://www.pbs.org/wonders/fr_cc.htm (accessed 22 November 2005)

◆ "On Africa," *National Geographic*, http://www.nationalgeographic.com/africa/ (accessed 3 November 2005)

◆ "The Story of Africa," BBC, http://www.bbc.co.uk/worldservice/africa/features/storyofafrica/ (accessed 22 November 2005)

Namibia

◆ "Namibia," http://www.globaladrenaline.com/africa/namibia/ (accessed 16 December 2005)

◆ "Namibia," http://www.exploreafrica.net/nam_geo.php (accessed 13 December 2005)

◆ "Namibia," *National Geographic*, http://www3.nationalgeographic.com/places/countries/country_namibia.html (accessed 13 December 2005)

◆ "Plants and Vegetation in Namibia," http://www.namibia-travel.net/namibia/flora.htm (accessed 16 December 2005)

◆ "Republic of Namibia," http://www.grnnet.gov.na/ (accessed 13 December 2005)

◆ "San," *Encylopaedia Britannica* online, http://www.britannica.com/ebc/article-9377634 (accessed 21 December 2005)

Malawi

◆ "About Malawain Culture," http://www.friendsofmalawi.org/learn_about_malawi/culture.html (accessed 15 December 2005)

◆ Friedson, Steven M., *Dancing Prophets: Musical Experience in Tumbuka Healing* (Chicago: University of Chicago Press, 1996)

◆ Kubik, Gerhard, "A Presentation of Kwela Music," *Scientific African* (4 March 2005), https://www.scientific-african.org/archives/kachamba/info8/view?searchterm=malawi (accessed 3 January 2006)

◆ "Malawi: Message in the Words," BBC, http://www.bbc.co.uk/worldservice/africa/features/rhythms/malawi.shtml (accessed 15 December 2005)

◆ "Malawi People and Culture," http://www.africaguide.com/country/malawi/culture.htm (accessed 15 December 2005)

◆ "Vimbuza Healing Dance," UNESCO, http://www.unesco.org/culture/intangible-heritage/21afr_uk.htm (accessed 6 January 2006)

Lesotho

◆ Byrnes, Rita M. (ed.), "Swazi, Sotho, and Ndebele States," http://countrystudies.us/south-africa/10.htm (accessed 3 January 2006)

◆ "Lesotho," http://www.lesotho.gov.ls/home/ (accessed 3 January 2006)

◆ "Lesotho," http://www.go2africa.com/lesotho/ (accessed 4 January 2006)

◆ "The Tswana," http://www.encounter.co.za/article/94.html (accessed 3 January 2006)

Swaziland

◆ "The Birth of Swaziland's Nature Conservation," http://www.biggameparks.org/conserv_birthofconservation.html (accessed 20 December 2005)

◆ Hall, James, "Poaching Declining in Swazliand," Spero News, http://www.speroforum.com/site/article.asp?id=1600 (accessed 20 December 2005)

◆ "The Ncwala First Fruits Festival of Swaziland," http://www.pilotguides.com/destination_guide/africa/south_africa_and_lesotho/ncwala.php (accessed 21 November 2005)

- "Swazi Culture," http://www.places.co.za/html/swazicul.html (accessed 21 November 2005)

- "Swaziland," Lonely Planet online, http://www.lonelyplanet.com/worldguide/destinations/africa/swaziland/ (accessed 21 November 2005)

Senegal

- "The Cultural Background," http://www.amadou.net/da/cultya.html (accessed 13 January 2006)

- "Sahel," PBS, http://www.pbs.org/wnet/africa/explore/sahel/sahel_overview.html (accessed 14 December 2005)

- "Senegal." http://www.africaguide.com/country/senegal/index.htm (accessed 12 January 2006)

- "Senegal," Lonely Planet online, http://www.lonelyplanet.com/worldguide/destinations/africa/senegal?poi=106013 (accessed 24 January 2006)

- "Senegal," *Columbia Encyclopedia* (6th edn, New York: Columbia University Press, 2001–5), http://www.bartleby.com/65/se/Senegal.html (accessed 24 January 2006)

Ghana

- "Drumming and Dancing in Ghana," http://www.ghanaexpeditions.com/main/index.asp (accessed 5 January 2006)

- "Field Guide to the Drums," http://www.drumsongstory.org/field_guide_to_the_drums.htm (accessed 6 January 2006)

- "Ghana," Microsoft® Encarta® Online Encyclopedia 2005, http://encarta.msn.com (© 1997–2005 Microsoft Corporation. All Rights Reserved)

- "Ghana People and Culture," http://www.africaguide.com/country/ghana/culture.htm (accessed 5 January 2006)

- McDermott, Gerald, *Anansi the Spider: A Tale from the Ashanti* New York: Holt, Rinehart and Winston, 1971)

- Stabbert, Jonette, "High Life in the Lowlands," http://www.expatica.com/actual/article.asp?subchannel_id=66&story_id=177 (accessed 5 January 2006)

Sudan

- Carney, Timothy, *Sudan: The Land and the People* (Washington: University of Washington Press, 2005)

- "Sudan," http://www.infoplease.com/ipa/A0107996).html (accessed 15 January 2006)

- "Sudan," *Columbia Enclopedia* (6th edn, New York: Columbia University Press, 2001–5), http://www.bartleby.com/65/su/Sudan.html (accessed 15 January 2006)

- "Sudan People and Society," Oxfam, http://www.oxfam.org.uk/coolplanet/kidsweb/world/sudan/sudpeop.htm (accessed 15 January 2006)

Ethiopia

- "Country Profile: Ethiopia," BBC, http://news.bbc.co.uk/1/hi/world/africa/country_profiles/1072164.stm (accessed 2 February 2006)

- "Ethiopia," Britannica Concise (*Britannica Concise Encylopedia* online), http://concise.britannica.com/ebc/article-9363950/Ethiopia (accessed 2 February 2006)

- "Food in Ethiopia," http://www.foodbycountry.com/Algeria-to-France/ Ethiopia.html (accessed 1 February 2006)

- Marcus, Harold G., *A History of Ethiopia* (California: University of California Press, 1994)

These pages contain African symbols in the artwork at the top and bottom. Each symbol has a special meaning: *Top, left to right:* Denkyem — adaptability and change; Odo nnyew fie kwan – love never loses its way home; Ananse ntontan — wisdom and creativity; Onyankopon adom nti briribiara beye yie — hope, faith and providence. *Bottom, left to right:* Fo fo — jealousy and envy; Dame-dame — intelligence and ingenuity; Mmusuyidee — good fortune and sanctity; Dwennimmen — humility and strength. The bullet points used throughout the book, like those on page 7, are the Ananse symbol.

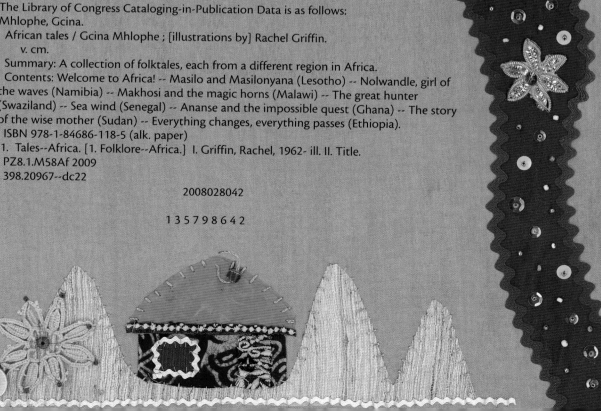

To my lovely daughter — G. M.
With love to my Mum and Dad — R. G.

The publisher would like to thank Diana Jeater, Professor of African History, University of the West of England, Bristol, for lending her academic expertise to this project.

Barefoot Books
2067 Massachusetts Avenue
Cambridge, MA 02140

This book has been printed on 100% acid-free paper

Color separation by Bright Arts, Singapore
Printed and bound in China by Printplus Ltd
This book was typeset in Cronos, Bembo, Catull and Umkhonto
The illustrations were created with embroidered collage on handmade papers

Hardcover ISBN 978-1-84686-118-5

The Library of Congress Cataloging-in-Publication Data is as follows:
Mhlophe, Gcina.
  African tales / Gcina Mhlophe ; [illustrations by] Rachel Griffin.
    v. cm.
  Summary: A collection of folktales, each from a different region in Africa.
  Contents: Welcome to Africa! -- Masilo and Masilonyana (Lesotho) -- Nolwandle, girl of
the waves (Namibia) -- Makhosi and the magic horns (Malawi) -- The great hunter
(Swaziland) -- Sea wind (Senegal) -- Ananse and the impossible quest (Ghana) -- The story
of the wise mother (Sudan) -- Everything changes, everything passes (Ethiopia).
  ISBN 978-1-84686-118-5 (alk. paper)
  1. Tales--Africa. [1. Folklore--Africa.] I. Griffin, Rachel, 1962- ill. II. Title.
  PZ8.1.M58Af 2009
  398.20967--dc22

               2008028042

            1 3 5 7 9 8 6 4 2

Barefoot Books
Celebrating Art and Story

At Barefoot Books, we celebrate art and story that opens
the hearts and minds of children from all walks of life, inspiring
them to read deeper, search further, and explore their own creative gifts.
Taking our inspiration from many different cultures, we focus on themes that
encourage independence of spirit, enthusiasm for learning, and sharing of
the world's diversity. Interactive, playful and beautiful, our products
combine the best of the present with the best of the past to
educate our children as the caretakers of tomorrow.

Live Barefoot!
Join us at www.barefootbooks.com